The Hair Scare

Story
Sujoyita Ghosh
Illustrations
Saumya Agrawal

Toto was almost ready to go to school
in his new winter uniform.
The blazer felt nice & warm.
But wait! There was something wrong.
It was his hair!It was long and messy,
growing in every possible direction.
Some standing straight like a broom,
and some curled up like the
sharpener shavings of a pencil.
It looked like a bird's nest!
Oh boy, what a thought!

Mamma had been trying to take him for a haircut
for the past two weeks, but he simply refused to go.
He wanted to grow his hair long
thinking it would make him look cool!
Mamma was terribly annoyed with him.
She kept trying to comb his hair
to make it look tidy.
But alas! That was not to be.
Grumbling, Mamma packed him off to school.

That afternoon,
Toto was walking
home with his friends
on his way back from school.
Suddenly a little bird came
and sat on his head.
It was a cuckoo!
Oh how Toto
and his friends loved it!
They thought it was great fun
and all of them walked quietly,
so the cuckoo wouldn't fly away.

When Toto reached home,
he tiptoed in and
signalled to his mother
that there was a
cuckoo sitting on his head.
But when Mamma peeked
into the messy hair,
she found no bird.
Instead, there were two little eggs!
They were greenish blue in colour
and had tiny dots all over.
The cuckoo had left
its eggs on Toto's head,
thinking it was a nice and cozy
nest!

Cuckoos always leave their eggs
in other birds' nests
and know that
the babies will soon hatch
under the care of the host bird.
The only thing different here
was that this was not a nest
but Toto's shaggy hair!

Mamma wanted to take the eggs
right away, but Toto insisted
on keeping them on his head,
little realising the inconvenience
it would cause him.
That night Toto slept
on a straight-backed wooden chair
so that the eggs
wouldn't fall off his hair.
Mamma switched on the radiator
so that Toto and the eggs
would be warm.

Toto was wide awake and very excited in the morning.
He had heard some chirping on his hair
and was waiting for his mother to come.
Mamma took a quick peek into Toto's hair
and found one little fledgling chirping furiously.
The little fellow seemed really hungry.
She rushed to the kitchen and got some porridge paste for it to eat.
She then stood and fed the baby bird, little by little.
Once fed, the baby cuckoo was nice and quiet.
It was only then, that Mamma noticed
the broken egg on the floor.

She then told Toto what must have happened.
Cuckoos are very clever birds.
The little fledgling upon hatching
had pushed out the other egg to make sure
that it got the parent's complete attention.
What a naughty and selfish little bird!

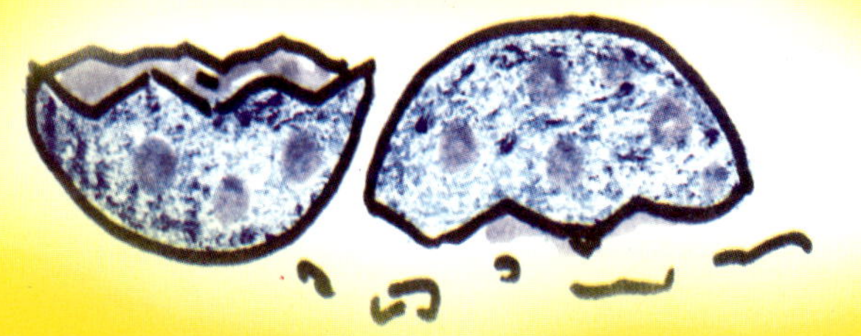

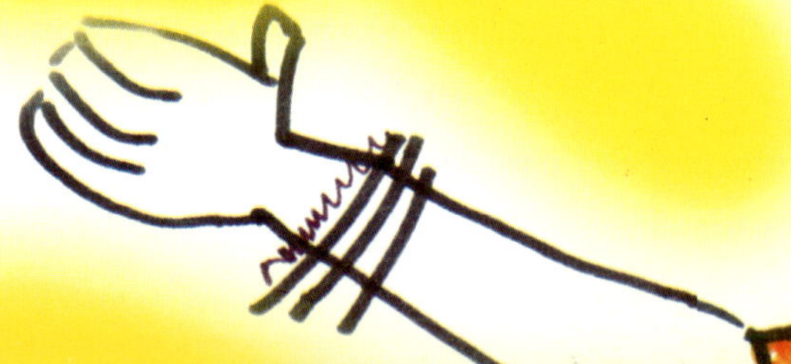

JULY
6

JULY
16

Days passed by but now Toto was completely exhausted.
He had slept on the straight-backed chair for ten days.
He longed for his own comfortable bed.
What was worse was that
he had not been able to go to school.
Imagine all the excitement he had missed out on!

The next morning, Mamma woke Toto up
and then gently nudged the baby cuckoo awake
and gave it some grains to eat — all on Toto's hair.
The baby bird woke up and
stretched itself, nice and long.
Then it began to peck on the grains
till its stomach was full.
This was really painful for Toto
since it often pecked hard on his head,
right through the hair.
Toto stood in front of the mirror
and glared at the bird.
The little cuckoo
seemed to be smirking at him!

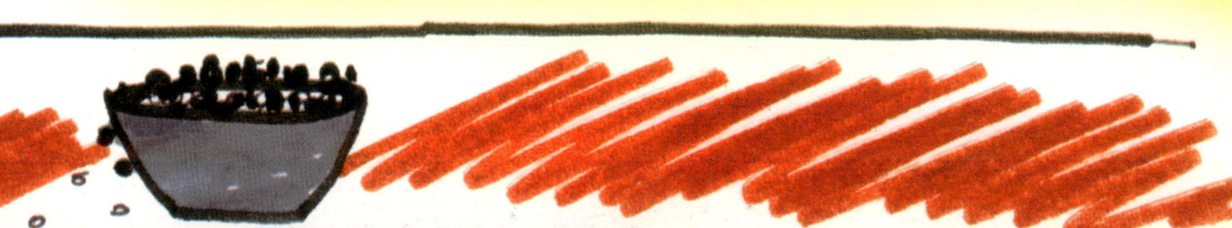

That afternoon,
when Toto was trying to take a nap
and Mamma was knitting,
the little cuckoo flew!

It landed on the sofa close by.
Again it flapped its wings
and did a full circle of the room.

Mamma woke Toto up and showed him the flying bird.
Toto jumped up with joy. He was thrilled to see the cuckoo flying as that meant freedom for him too. He ran to the window and opened it wide. The little bird flew to Mamma's shoulder and perched itself as if to say *thank you* and then flew out of the window into the garden.
It turned towards Toto once and chirruped again.

Toto had learnt his lesson. He turned to his mother and said, "Mamma, we are going for a haircut right away. Please take me. And this time I want a crew-cut, like the soldiers. No more birds laying eggs on *my* head!"

Activities

Spot six differences in the two pictures.

Only one of the pictures numbered 2 follows the sequence of the story. Circle the correct picture.